Donny   Davy   KiKi   Eddie

Copyright © 2008 by NordSüd Verlag AG, Zürich, Switzerland.
First published in Switzerland under the title *Pauli Fußballstar*.
English translation copyright © 2008 by North-South Books Inc., New York.

First published in the United States, Great Britain, Canada, Australia,
and New Zealand in 2008 by North-South Books, an imprint of
NordSüd Verlag AG, Zürich, Switzerland.

Distributed in the United States by North-South Books Inc., New York.

Library of Congress Cataloging-in-Publication Data is available.
A CIP catalog record for this book is available from The British Library.

ISBN 978-0-7358-2196-5
10 9 8 7 6 5 4 3 2 1

Printed in Belgium

www.northsouth.com

DAVY,
Soccer Star!

By Brigitte Weninger
Illustrated by Eve Tharlet

New York / London

Davy and Eddie chased Grandpa's funny old soccer ball across the yard. The old cloth ball was so worn and torn, Davy wondered how many more kicks it could take.

"Here it comes, Kiki!" shouted Davy. Kiki was playing goalie between two clothesline poles.

WHAP! Up the ball soared, over the goalposts . . .

. . . and right into a big thorny bush.

R-R-R-R-RIP!

"Oh, no!" cried Davy. "It's all undone! How can we play with a ball that's as flat as a pancake?" He gave the lump of cloth a kick.

"That won't help," said Kiki. "Let's see if your mother can mend it."

But when Mother saw the torn scraps of cloth, she shook her head. "I can sew, but I can't do magic," she said. "I'm afraid this old ball has had it."

"*Now* what will we do?" Davy moaned. "No ball, no soccer."

Father looked up from his newspaper. "Guess what I've been reading?" he said. "The Big Bad Badgers have announced a Soccer Challenge Game. Anyone who can beat them gets a trophy—*and* a brand new ball just like the pros use."

"That's it!" shouted Davy. "Where do we sign up?"

"Wait a minute," said Eddie. "We're not good enough."

"The Big Bad Badgers are really great," said Kiki.

"Badgers Smadgers!" Davy shouted. "We can do it. We'll practice. We're going to be soccer stars!"

By evening, Davy had his team. He was captain. Kiki was goalie.
The other players gathered around while Kiki counted, "Eddie . . .
Dan . . . Donny . . . Daisy. . . . That makes six. We need one more."

Davy looked down at his little sister. "Dinah can do it," he said.
"She's little, but she's fast."

"YIPPEEEE!" Dinah flung her arms around Davy's neck. "I'm a wild soccer rabbit!"

"Good name," said Davy. "We'll be the Wild Rabbits against the Big Bad Badgers." He punched the air with his fist. *"And who's going to win?"*

"We are! We are! We are!" everyone shouted.

Eddie held up his hand. "Er . . . there's just one problem," he said. "We don't have a ball."

"I have an idea," said Father. He rummaged around in his shed. Finally he pulled out an old leather pouch.

Mother stuffed the old cloth ball into the pouch and sewed the opening up tight. "It looks a little lumpy," she said.

"That's all right, Mother," said Davy. "It's good enough for practice. Pretty soon we'll have a ball just like the pros use."

The next morning, Davy got his team going early. They started with a cross country run. Then they did push-ups and jumping jacks. Afterwards they practiced kicking and passing and guarding.

When they finally took a break, Dinah was limping. "Owww," she moaned. "I have a charley cow in my leg."

Mother laughed. "It's called a charley *horse*. A little rubbing will make it better."

Mother took care of everyone's aches and pains. Father cleared a new field for the team. Eddie's and Kiki's mothers made berry juice and spinach balls for energy. Everybody was feeling the team spirit.

A few days later, the Wild Rabbits were off on their early morning run. As they raced around a curve in the path, they almost crashed into the Big Bad Badgers.

"Watch where you're going!" shouted Boris Badger.

"Hey, Long Ears," sneered Bixby Badger. "Aren't you the little twerps who think you can beat us?"

"What a joke!" Bubba Badger snickered. "They even have *girls* on their team."

"Girls are just as good at soccer as boys!" Daisy shouted.

The Badgers ran off laughing.

"See you soon, Bunny Babies!" they called back. "We're gonna wipe you off the field!"

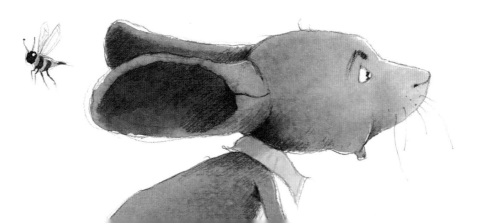

"Did you see those muscles?" Dan whispered.

Donny nodded. "And those legs! They'll kick us to the moon."

"Okay, listen up," said Davy. "We're the Wild Rabbits! We play like pros. Are we gonna let a bunch of badger bullies walk away with *our new ball?*"

"No way!" shouted Kiki. "Who's going to win that ball?"

"Wild Rabbits!" shouted Dinah.

Pretty soon everyone was shouting. "Wild Rabbits! Wild Rabbits! Wild Rabbits!"

Day after day, the Wild Rabbits worked and ran and practiced. They ate spinach balls until they felt green.

When the big day arrived at last, everyone felt a little nervous. They were about to leave for the soccer field when Mother hurried up. "We have a surprise for our team," she said. She passed out a beautiful red uniform to each player.

"Wow!" said Davy. "Now we look like a real team. Let's go play like one!"

When Davy and the Wild Rabbits marched into the stadium, their new red uniforms flashed in the sun. Everyone clapped and cheered. Max the Mole blew the starting whistle and the game began.

The Big Bad Badgers scored the first goal. The Wild Rabbits bounced right back with a goal by Captain Davy. "Way to go, Davy!" shouted fans in the stands.

The Badgers were strong, and their kicks were powerful. But the Wild Rabbits were clever, and their morning runs had made them fast. Even little Dinah dribbled the ball away right from under a badger's nose. When the badger thought no one was watching, he kicked Dinah so hard he sent her spinning. Davy ran to help her up.

TWEEEEET went the whistle. Penalty against the Big Bad Badgers! Dinah would get a free penalty kick.

"Don't worry," said Davy. "I'll do the kick for you."

"I'll do it myself!" said Dinah. She wiped away her tears.

Dinah set up the ball, took a run-up with lightning speed, kicked the ball with all her might—and sent it flying right past the flabbergasted Badger goalie.

GOAL! Final whistle! The Wild Rabbits had won!

The crowd roared and cheered.

Captain Davy carried Dinah off the field on his shoulders.

The Wild Rabbits were presented with a big trophy cup. And there it was at last: a brand-new, beautiful soccer ball, just like the pros use. Davy held it up for all his team to see.

"Practice first thing in the morning," said Captain Davy, "with our *new* ball! See you tomorrow, Wild Rabbit Champions!"